# WHAT THE GAME IS ALL ABOUT—TEAM BALL!

Will cut quickly across the court from the right side toward the center of the lane. Doug and Sam raced around the perimeter, bringing two Slashers outside. Dave faked toward Doug, then fired a lightning-fast bounce pass into Will's hands.

Just as Will figured, three Slashers swarmed on him. At the last possible moment, he turned and lobbed the ball over their heads to Brian, who was standing open at the left side of the baseline. Doug and Sam had lured the rest of the Slashers out of the play. With plenty of time, Brian squared up and delivered a flawless jumper.

Don't miss any of the books in

—a slammin', jammin', in-your-face action series,
new from Bantam Books!

#1 Crashing the Boards
#2 In Your Face!

Coming soon:
#3 Trash Talk

# CRASHING
# THE BOARDS

### by
## Hank Herman

BANTAM BOOKS
NEW YORK · TORONTO · LONDON · SYDNEY · AUCKLAND

RL 2.6, 007-010

CRASHING THE BOARDS
*A Bantam Book / February 1996*

Produced by Daniel Weiss Associates, Inc.
*33 West 17th Street*
*New York, NY 10011*

*Cover art by Jeff Mangiat*

*All rights reserved.*

**Copyright © 1996 by Daniel Weiss Associates, Inc., and
Daniel Ehrenhaft.**

ISBN: 0-553-48273-4

*Published simultaneously in the United States and Canada*

*Bantam Books are published by Bantam Books, a division of Bantam
Doubleday Dell Publishing Group, Inc. Its trademark, consisting of the
words "Bantam Books" and the portrayal of a rooster, is Registered in U.S.
Patent and Trademark Office and in other countries. Marca Registrada.
Bantam Books, 1540 Broadway, New York, New York 10036.*

PRINTED IN THE UNITED STATES OF AMERICA

OPM     0 9 8 7

*Respectfully dedicated to Matt "The Cap'n" Viverito.*

"Let's go, Bulls!" Will Hopwood yelled.

Will was guarding Matt Johnstone near the top of the key. Suddenly Matt faked to his right, then pivoted on his left foot and threw up a fadeaway jump shot.

The ball sailed over the tips of Will's hands. It bounced off the backboard and fell into the net.

"Nice! Let's play some D now," said Otto Meyerson as he ran back on defense. "Tie game. Next basket wins."

Will wiped the sweat off his forehead and glared in the mean-looking kid's direction. It figured Otto was trying to cheat.

"No way!" Will shouted. "Win by two."

Otto's pudgy face wrinkled into a frown. "C'mon! It's almost seven-thirty, man. We've been playing for hours. I'm about to pass out!"

Will stood up straight and stared at Otto. At five feet two, Will was the tallest player on the Branford Bulls. His size came in handy when he wanted guys like Otto to shut up.

"Then score two baskets," he replied. "That's the rule."

"The rule?" Otto smirked. He looked around the playground. "I don't see a ref."

Will decided to ignore him. He knew that Otto and the rest of the Slashers would keep playing. After all, this wasn't just any old pickup game. The two teams had been talking about having this five-on-five grudge match, on the Bulls' court and without refs, since last fall—and it was already June.

Last summer, Will had turned nine. That meant he was finally old enough to play for his hometown of Branford in Danville County's summer basketball league.

With Will starting at center, the Branford Bulls had gone all the way to the September championship. But they had lost. Even worse, they had been cheated out of a victory by the Sampton Slashers.

Will gritted his teeth, remembering the game. It had been awful. The ref had called hardly any fouls against Sampton. Later, Will found out from Coach McBane that the ref and the Slashers' coach were brothers. There was *no* way Will was going to let this game go because Otto Meyerson was tired.

"Let's take it to 'em, Bulls!" he shouted.

He called his teammates into a quick huddle before they checked the ball.

"Brian, try to get open at the left side of the baseline," he whispered. "Dave, feed the ball to me inside, and I'll kick it back out to Brian for the jumper."

Brian Simmons and David Danzig grinned at each other. The baseline was Brian's sweet spot on the court. In fact, Will couldn't remember a single day Brian had left Branford's Jefferson Park playground without sinking five baseline jumpers in a row. If Brian had the ball there, the Bulls were almost guaranteed a bucket!

Will also knew that the Slashers wouldn't expect him to pass to Brian. *Those ballhogs don't know anything about playing team ball,* Will said to himself with a chuckle.

Everyone on the Slashers—especially Otto—wanted the glory of driving to the hoop alone. If Otto had the ball inside the lane, he would always barrel toward the basket and put up a shot. His moves were good enough to fake out a lot of players, but he would just as often get stuffed.

Defensively, they would always double- or triple-team anyone who had the ball within ten feet of the basket. And that always left most of their opponents wide open.

"Doug and Sam, you guys draw the rest of the defense outside," Will added, before heading out on the court.

The McBane twins nodded at the same time. Will didn't know of any brothers who were more alike—or better at hoops. But that wasn't surprising. After all, Coach McBane was their father.

"We'll have them running in circles," said Sam as he and the other boys joined Will on the court.

4

"They won't know what hit 'em," said Doug, inbounding the ball to Dave.

"Time to show these fools what's up," said Dave, brushing his long blond bangs out of his eyes.

Will grinned. Dave dribbled the ball between his legs as he took it downcourt, just to show off. But Will could tell Dave's eyes were sizing up the Slashers' defense.

The moment Dave hit the top of the key, the Bulls hustled into action. Will felt a surge of confidence. This was what the game was all about! Team ball.

Will cut quickly across the court from the right side toward the center of the lane. Doug and Sam raced around the perimeter, bringing two Slashers outside. Dave faked toward Doug, then fired a lightning-fast bounce pass into Will's hands.

Just as Will figured, three Slashers swarmed on him. At the last possible moment, he turned and lobbed the ball over their heads to Brian, who was standing open at the left side of the baseline. Doug and Sam had lured the rest of the

Slashers out of the play. With plenty of time, Brian squared up and delivered a flawless jumper.

"Yesss!" cried Dave, doing his best Marv Albert imitation.

Brian smiled and ran his hand over his short fade haircut. "Nothin' but net."

Will high-fived Brian as the Bulls rushed back on D. "Win by two," he called.

"Yeah, yeah. We know. The rules." Otto was dribbling the ball slowly upcourt. He had an angry look on his face. Dave came out to guard him. Suddenly Otto faked to his left and bolted past Dave toward the basket.

Will concentrated hard as Otto came rushing at him down the lane. In that split second, Will saw that Otto wasn't paying attention; he was busy eyeing the basket. As Otto went up for the shot, Will deftly reached in and stripped the ball from his hands.

Dave took off, sprinting upcourt alone. Will hurled an overhand pass to him, Hail

Mary style. The ball flew across the length of the court and landed right in Dave's hands. *Yes!* He sped toward the hoop.

Will watched anxiously as Dave dribbled once behind his back, and then put up a crazy reverse layup that completely missed the basket.

*What the heck was he doing?* Luckily, nobody else had even crossed the half-court line yet.

"Oops!" Dave quickly got his own rebound and banked an easy shot off the board.

"Yes!" shouted Brian. He ran downcourt and met Dave in mid-leap, swinging his arm around to slap Dave's hand down low—the Bulls' trademark victory "low five."

"Sweet!" yelled Sam.

"Revenge!" shouted Doug.

Will laughed as he low-fived Doug and Sam. Winning the grudge match felt great. "Nothing's gonna stop us now, guys!" Will yelled, putting his arms around the twins. "You can tell your dad we're taking the title home this year!"

# CHAPTER 2

For some reason, Doug and Sam McBane didn't look as psyched as Will expected they would.

Oh, well. Maybe they were just tired. It *was* late.

Will turned around to shake hands with the Slashers. "Great game," he said to Otto.

Otto just stared at Will's outstretched arm with a sour look on his face. The rest of the Slashers gathered around. Otto turned to a tall, lanky kid with long stringy hair. "Yo, Spider. Check it out—a real sportsman."

He turned back to Will with a big, fake

smile. "Great game, sport," he said loudly. He reached out to shake Will's hand, then pulled back at the last second, running his hand through his greasy brown hair instead. "Psych."

Spider snickered.

By this time, Dave and Brian had walked over. Will knew that Dave had a very short temper—especially when it came to morons like Otto.

"I think that move went out in the eighties, dude," Dave said. Then he grinned. *"Psych."*

Otto stepped forward. He looked tough. He looked like the kind of kid who liked to pick fights.

"You got a problem?" he asked Dave.

"Only with your breath."

*Uh-oh.* Will quickly stepped between them. "Yo—chill out." He turned to Otto. "Look, man, if you don't want to shake my hand, that's cool. Just don't bother coming back to Jefferson. We'll see you on the courts this season."

"What, you own this dump?"

"Yeah, we do, actually," said Dave. "And we don't like trespassers. So get lost."

"My pleasure," Otto muttered. "I wouldn't come back here if you paid me." He looked around the playground. "I mean, maybe if you had a *real* court . . ." Suddenly he slapped his forehead with his palm. "Oops—I forgot! Branford doesn't have any real courts—it only has a beat-up playground."

Will started to open his mouth, but had nothing to say. Otto was right. Branford *was* the only town in the league that didn't have a community center. The Bulls had to practice at Jefferson Park and play all their games on the road.

"Oh, well." Otto shrugged. "I guess you have to deal with it."

"Sort of like your face," said Dave. "I mean, it must be hard when your face looks like a dog's butt—but you deal with it."

Otto ignored Dave's comment. "We'll see you guys when you come to Sampton," he said. "But then again, maybe not. I don't know if security will let scrubs like you inside."

"Oh, yeah, that's right," Brian said. "They only let Slashers' relatives inside. Like your refs."

Otto narrowed his eyes at Brian. He turned to leave. "C'mon, guys, we're outta here."

"'Bye, scrubs!" yelled Spider as the Slashers left the playground.

Doug shook his head. "Man, those guys are pathetic."

"Yeah," Brian said. "I guess they know we're going to crush them this season. That's why they're acting so lame."

"Of course we're going to crush them," Dave said. "Unless they get Otto's uncle to call the games," he added with a lopsided smile.

Will started laughing. "It wouldn't even matter. We're gonna crush them, and on *their* court."

Dave picked up the ball and started twirling it on his finger. Will looked at Brian and rolled his eyes. Dave never passed up an opportunity to show off.

"Sampton's defense stinks," Dave said as the ball spun around and around. "Come to think of it, so does Plainview's, Rochester's, and every other team's. They don't have a chance. That's all there is to it."

*"Show time!"* Brian and Will yelled at

11

the same time, exchanging a low five.

Will looked over at Sam and Doug McBane. They had been standing quietly. "Maybe we should get your mom to ref," he cracked. "Then we'd be sure to win the championship."

The twins didn't say anything. They weren't even smiling. In fact, they suddenly looked a little gloomy.

"Yo, cheer up, guys," Dave said. "We just beat the Slashers!"

Doug and Sam looked at each other. "Uh . . . right," Doug said finally.

"*And* we're gonna rock this season," Will added. "Aren't you guys psyched?"

"Uh—yeah, sure," said Sam. He and Doug looked at each other again, then quickly looked away.

"Let's go to Bowman's," mumbled Doug. "I'm kinda thirsty."

"To Bowman's!" yelled Dave, taking one last wild hook shot from mid-court. "Oops," he said as the ball bounced out the front gate. "Remind me not to do that in the championship."

"Hey, guys," Sam suddenly blurted out. He looked at the ground. "Before

12

you get too psyched about the championship, Doug and I have something we
need to tell you. Our dad got a new job
on the West Coast. We're leaving in two
weeks."

"*What!*"

# CHAPTER 3

Before Will could say anything, the McBanes' car pulled up in front of Jefferson. Coach McBane got out and slammed the door. "From the looks of all the long faces, I'd guess that Sam and Doug told you the news," he said.

"What the heck is going on?" Will demanded.

"To be honest, Will, I wasn't sure myself that we'd be leaving until only a few days ago. Everything has happened so fast. I know it doesn't seem fair to you guys. I feel terrible."

"But you can't leave," Dave said. "We

14

just won our grudge match against the Slashers. We need you this season!"

Coach McBane shook his head. "I'm really sorry. I wish the boys and I could all stay, but we can't."

"At least we beat the Slashers together," Doug said.

"Yeah," said Sam. "And you guys will find more players. Not as good as us, maybe, but that would be impossible."

Everyone laughed, but it didn't make Will feel any better about the McBanes' leaving. He watched as Sam and Doug slid silently into the backseat of their car. Coach McBane got in and rolled down the window.

"I just want you to know that I think you are a great bunch of ballplayers," Coach McBane said. "You're going to have plenty of better coaches in your life and play on lots of teams. You'll see, you'll just keep getting better." He started to roll up the window and then stopped. "Oh, and, guys? I want you all to come to a good-bye barbecue we're having on Tuesday."

"Thanks, Coach, we'll be there," Will replied glumly.

"Great. So we'll see you then." Coach McBanc rolled up the window. The car disappeared down the street.

Will and his friends stood watching in stunned silence.

"This bites," said Dave finally.

Will shook his head. "That's the understatement of the year."

"Well, if it isn't Too Tall. What can I do for you, my man?"

Mr. Bowman had a nickname for almost every kid in Branford. He had started calling Will "Too Tall" last summer because Will had grown four inches the year before.

"We just beat Sampton in a preseason rematch of the championship," Will replied glumly. He grabbed a bunch of Cokes from the refrigerator in the rear of the store and walked  back up front. He dumped them down on the counter in front of Mr. Bowman. "The victory bash is on me."

Bowman's market was right across the street from Jefferson Park. The Bulls ended almost every practice with a soda in front of the store.

"Nice work, Too Tall. All that slackin' and goofin' off this winter must have paid off." Mr. Bowman looked out the window at Dave and Brian waiting on the bench. "Whew—Droopy and Fadeaway look winded. You guys had better start doing some cross-training," he said with a smile.

Mr. Bowman called Dave "Droopy" because Dave's long blond hair hung in his face and he always wore cut-off shorts that came down to his knees. Brian was called "Fadeaway" because he was known at Jefferson for his fadeaway jump shot— and because he had a fade haircut exactly like Scottie Pippen's.

"We don't have to worry about cross-training," muttered Will. "I don't know if we even have a team anymore."

"What?" Mr. Bowman's eyes widened.

"I'm too depressed to talk about it now."

Mr. Bowman nodded. "I understand. But if you want to talk or need some advice, I'll be here."

17

It was a nice thing to say, and Mr. Bowman *had* given the Bulls lots of good advice in the past. Mr. Bowman was a chubby, balding, African American man in his mid-fifties. He didn't look like much of a ballplayer anymore, but Will knew he had been drafted by the New York Knicks out of college. An injury had kept him from a professional basketball career. Still, Will couldn't see Mr. Bowman helping much now.

"Thanks." Will paid for the sodas and joined Dave and Brian. They were still talking about the game.

"The thing about Otto is that he's a good player," Dave was saying. "He's got a good shot and he's a good ball handler. But he could be *great*. I mean, I know the Slashers' faces are painful to look at, but I don't think I saw the kid pass the ball during the whole game."

"I think he tried once," said Brian. "Oh, no—I remember now. It was just an air ball that happened to hit Spider in the head."

"Hmmm, trash talk," a deep voice interrupted. "The telltale sign of a win."

Will looked up to see Mr. Bowman's

son, Nate, rounding the corner. Nate was a tall seventeen-year-old with a wide smile and a hoop earring. "Now, don't be getting too bigheaded before the season even starts," he joked, grinning and running his hand over his closely cut hair. "Overconfidence can be a player's biggest weakness. Take it from a professional."

WOW! size 13!

Will rolled his eyes. Nate Bowman was something of a legend at Jefferson. Not only could he slam-dunk, but he wore an unbelievable size-thirteen shoe. He was also one of the starting guards for the local high school's varsity basketball team. The other was Jim Hopwood—Will's sixteen-year-old brother.

"Jim told me about the grudge match you guys were having today," said Nate. He looked at his watch. "Man, it's almost eight! Must have been a long game."

"It was," said Will, trying to sound excited. "But we showed 'em what's up. It was the easiest game we ever played."

Nate laughed. "That's the spirit, Too Tall. Forget what I said about overconfidence. It doesn't apply in your case."

Suddenly there was a knock on the window of the shop. Mr. Bowman was gesturing impatiently for Nate to come in. Nate looked annoyed. "Man, it's going to be a long summer," he said. "I'm going to have to work here five days a week and help close up on the weekends. All work and no play." He shrugged and opened the door. "See you all later."

Will, Dave, and Brian fell silent.

"What are we going to do without Coach McBane?" Brian suddenly blurted. "Where are we going to get another coach as good as he is? Where are we going to find a coach at all?"

"That's not our only problem," said Will. "We just lost two of our starters. I don't even know if the rest of the team plans to play this summer."

Dave nodded miserably. "Let's face it— the Bulls are through."

# CHAPTER 4

"Left-handed hook, nothin' but net," called Dave. He put up the shot from the right side of the key. Will watched blankly as the ball sailed over the court and plopped into the net with a swish. Dave smiled. "Now let's see you chumps make that one."

Will took the ball and stood where Dave had made the shot. He stared gloomily at the basket. "Horse is a dumb game," he muttered.

"I thought you loved horse," Brian said.

Will just shrugged. "I used to. But that was when we had a team."

His shot fell three feet short of the hoop.

"Well, that spells h-o-r-s-e for you, my man," said Dave.

"Who cares? It's not like it matters anymore."

A week had passed since they had said good-bye to the McBanes at the barbecue. Meanwhile, Will, Brian, and Dave hadn't had any luck finding another coach. Even worse, Coach McBane had told their league that he was leaving. The Bulls were officially finished.

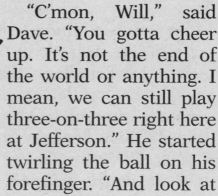

"C'mon, Will," said Dave. "You gotta cheer up. It's not the end of the world or anything. I mean, we can still play three-on-three right here at Jefferson." He started twirling the ball on his forefinger. "And look at it this way—no more free-throw drills."

"Three-on-three isn't like playing on a real team, and you know it," Will said shortly. "It doesn't even come close."

"Hey, you know what?" Brian piped up. "I ran into Pete Bonilla yesterday. He told me he was going to Essex today to try out for the Eagles."

"Really?" Dave chuckled. "Well, he shouldn't have any problem making the cut. Of course the worst team in the league would want the worst player in the league!"

Will grinned. Pete had been the second-string small forward for the Bulls last summer. Everyone on the team had liked him a lot, but he was a total klutz on the court.

"Do you think Essex will let him play even if he lives in Branford?" Will asked.

"I guess so," Brian said. "Why not?"

"Hmmm," said Will. "I'm just thinking. All the league tryouts are today, right?"

"That's what Pete said."

Dave stopped twirling the ball on his finger. "What are you getting at, Will?"

Will suddenly felt excited. "I think Pete had the right idea. He just went to the wrong place. We've been looking forward all year to beating the Slashers this season, right? Well, if we can't beat 'em as the Bulls—we'll join 'em."

"Are you serious?" cried Brian. "Are you saying we should try out for the Slashers?"

23

Dave laughed. "Will, you're a genius! Of course we should try out for the Slashers. What could be sweeter than benching their starters?"

"Exactly," said Will. "We go to Sampton and show those fools what's up—and then we take over their team." He clapped his hands together. "Piece of cake!"

Dave dribbled once and threw up a turnaround jumper. It dropped straight through the net. "Yeah, I don't think we'll have much of a problem, do you?"

"Remember, crash the boards and box out," said Jim Hopwood when he dropped Will, Brian, and Dave off in front of the Sampton community center. "Any dummy can make a shot, but good, tough D is what really impresses a coach."

Will watched his brother drive away. The last time Will had been in Sampton, the Bulls had lost the championship. He was suddenly nervous.

"Well, what are we waiting for?" asked Brian. "It's show time."

The three of them walked into the gym. Will glanced at the court. The Slashers' starters were playing a bunch of confused-looking kids who had come for the try-outs. Most of them could barely dribble, much less make a basket.

Dave snickered. "This is gonna be no problem," he said.

Mr. White, the Slashers' coach, was sitting on the bench watching the game. He was a tall, pale man with curly red hair and a beard.

"Well, hello there," Coach White said when he saw them. "Long time no see. Hey—I heard about what happened. Tough break." He shook his head and turned back to the game.

There was a long silence.

"We've come to try out for the Slashers," Will finally said.

Coach White laughed. "Very funny."

"What's so funny about it?" Brian asked.

"C'mon, you guys. I don't have time for this."

Dave laughed. "By the looks of those dopes out on your court, you should have been praying that we'd show up."

Coach White shot a quick look at Dave. "I don't like your tone, son. You'd better watch it when you're on my court."

"He didn't mean it like that, Coach White," said Will. "We just want a fair shot at making the Slashers, like everyone else."

"You're serious, aren't you?" he asked, looking Will in the eye. "You're not here to cause trouble?"

"No, sir," Will replied. "You know that we don't have a team anymore. We're here to try out. Honest."

"Well . . . okay. If you guys really mean it . . ." Coach White stood up and blew the whistle that was hanging around his neck. The piercing sound echoed through the gym. Everyone stopped playing and walked over to the bench.

"Hey—it's the Branford Butt-heads!" shouted Otto when he saw them. "I'm sorry. I shouldn't call you that. Branford doesn't have a team anymore. From now on, I'll just call you the Butt-heads."

"Quiet, Otto," said Coach White. "All right, boys. We've got some late arrivals, so we're going to change things up a little. Otto, Spider, Matt—I want you guys to play a quick half-court three-on-three to five with our friends from Branford here. Let's go!" He blew the whistle loudly.

"Jeez," whispered Brian. "If he blows that whistle one more time, I think I'm gonna go deaf."

Otto checked the ball with Dave to start the game.

"I can't believe you guys are trying out for the Slashers," Otto said as he dribbled downcourt. He sounded surprised, but determined. "You haven't got a prayer."

As usual, Otto immediately tried to take the ball to the basket himself. Will ran over to help Dave on defense, double-teaming Otto inside the lane. As Otto went up for a shot, Will jumped up and got a piece of the ball. It glanced off the backboard and fell back into Will's hands.

"Nice!" shouted Brian.

Will passed off the ball to Dave for an easy layup.

"Come on, Slashers!" yelled Coach White. "Move the ball around. More passing, Otto!"

Otto took the ball in at the top of the key and whipped it to Matt. Just as Matt

27

was about to pass, Brian stripped the ball from him. Coach White blew his whistle.

"Foul!" he called. "Slashers' ball."

Will shook his head. Brian hadn't touched Matt. Coach White had made a bad call so the Slashers could get the ball back. *Just like the championship,* Will thought.

Otto was able to score on a quick give-and-go to Spider when the Slashers inbounded the ball.

"I can't believe Coach White is being a jerk in tryouts," Dave said to Will. "It's not even a real game."

"Just chill," Will said. "We're still going to win."

The next time the Slashers had the ball, Will intercepted one of Otto's passes and took the ball into the lane himself for the layup. Before the ball even hit the floor, Will yelled, "Back to D!"

Brian and Dave sprinted to cover Spider and Matt before Otto could inbound. Otto looked desperately from one teammate to the other. He knew he couldn't make a decent pass to either of them. Brian and Dave were glued to

Spider's and Matt's every move.

Finally Otto tried to lob the ball over Brian's head to Spider. Brian easily picked it off. He dribbled once and planted both feet on the ground. Spider jumped in front of him in a last-second effort to block his shot. As Spider went down, Brian leaped up, delivering his famous fadeaway jump shot. It bounced squarely off the backboard and fell in.

"Sweetness," said Dave, giving Brian a low five. "Three to one."

Just then Coach White blew his whistle. "All right, all right, I've seen enough," he called. "Let's wrap it up here."

Everyone gathered around the bench.

"Well, Coach White, if we can do this against your starters, we can probably do pretty well in a real game," Will said confidently.

"Yeah," mumbled Dave. "Imagine what we could do for the Slashers if there was a ref who didn't cheat."

Coach White glared at him. "What was that, son?"

"Oh, nothing," said Dave innocently.

*C'mon, Dave*, Will said to himself. *I*

*know Coach White is a jerk—but don't mess it up for the rest of us.*

"Well, it's clear you three know how to play basketball. You all have good shooting, passing, and ball-handling skills. You hustle on defense." Coach White looked around the bench. "And I'm glad to see all the rest of you who came down to give it your best. Unfortunately, though, I have room for only one player—and that's Will Hopwood. The Slashers need a starting center."

*What!* Will couldn't believe it. After all that, he had made the Slashers and his two best friends hadn't.

He looked at Brian and Dave. They were staring at the gym floor, looking like two sad dogs with their tails between their legs. The rest of the kids who didn't make the team were already filing out of the gym.

"So what do you say, Hopwood? You in?"

Will hated to leave Dave and Brian out in the cold. But he *had* waited all winter to play basketball—real basketball on a real team. Now he had the chance.

"Go ahead, Will," said Dave, looking up.

He tried to smile. "You want to play team ball, don't you?"

"And you want to go to the championship—right?" Brian asked.

The championship! Will took a look around at Otto, Spider, and the rest of the Slashers. Sure, they looked and acted like morons. But they *were* a good team.

And with the Bulls gone, they would probably win more games than any other team in the league.

"All right, Coach White," he said finally. "I'm in!"

# CHAPTER 5

Will stood perfectly still at mid-court, poised for the jump ball. His heart felt as if it were about to leap out of his chest. This is what he had been waiting for all year.

The ref was new to the league, a kid about Nate and Jim's age. The ref glanced first at Will, then at the Harrison Hornets' opposing center. Everyone in the gym was silent. Finally he blew the whistle and tossed the ball up in the air. The season had begun!

Will's Reeboks made a loud screech on the court as he leaped up and batted the ball to Matt. Matt dribbled the ball quickly downcourt. Will saw Spider sprinting to-ward thc basket.

Matt put up what looked at first like a bad shot. Suddenly Spider caught the ball in mid-air, dribbled once, and banked in the layup.

The gym exploded with cheering.

*Jeez, what a play!* Will was amazed.

"Come on, guys," Coach White yelled as they ran back on defense. "We have all season to show off. Let's stick to what we practiced, all right?"

"Sampton two, Harrison zero," announced a deep voice over the gym's loudspeaker.

The Slashers were playing their first game at home against the Harrison Hornets. Will noticed that the gym was packed with spectators. His pulse was rac-ing. This was it! Real ball on a real team.

*"De-fense, de-fense, de-fense,"* chanted the crowd.

The Hornets worked the ball around the perimeter. Will guarded the Hornets'

center, a big kid with braces. The center was trying to muscle his way past Will toward the basket.

Suddenly one of the Hornets' guards put up a shot from the right side of the court. Will quickly spun around to face the hoop. As the ball teetered on the rim, Will could feel the Hornets' center trying to get around him for the rebound—but Will was able to box him out. He jumped high to meet the ball and grabbed it with both hands.

"Nice D, Hopwood," shouted a familiar voice. "Way to hustle."

Will dished the ball off to Otto and looked up into the bleachers. He couldn't believe his eyes. It was Dave! He was standing in the top row with his fist raised and a wide smile on his face. And next to him was Brian, and Will's brother, Jim!

Now Will was twice as psyched to play a great game.

As Otto took the ball downcourt, Will dashed into the lane and began posting up on the Hornets' center. Otto dribbled the ball around the perimeter.

Just when Will had pushed his way to a spot right under the hoop, Otto threw up a shot from deep outside. The ball bounced off the rim. As it fell to the floor, Will leaped up, caught it, and swished it before his feet even touched the ground.

"*Yesss!*" shouted the crowd.

"Time out," called Coach White.

Will gathered with the rest of the Slashers around the bench.

"Let's move the ball around a little more out there," said Coach White. "More passing means more open shots. We're doing well, but we could have more points on the board."

The Slashers headed back onto the court. "Man, Coach White is starting to sound like a broken record," Otto grumbled. "'More passing.' Why doesn't he just shut up and let us play?"

"Maybe he's right, Otto," said Will. "Maybe we should try to do what he says."

"Nobody asked you, Hopwood." Otto glared at Will. "Remember, we have to play together, but I don't have to like you."

Will felt the same way, but just shrugged and let it slide. If he opened his mouth, he knew he would probably end up getting into a fight with Otto.

The Slashers quickly jumped out to a 10–4 lead in the first quarter.

As the quarter drew to a close, Otto took the ball downcourt. The Hornets had started using a two–one–two zone defense to keep the Slashers from penetrating inside the lane. Jim had once told Will that the biggest weakness of a zone defense was that it couldn't stop a good passing game. So while Otto dribbled the ball around the perimeter, Will hustled to the inside, trying to get open for a pass.

The clock ticked down. Will quickly found an open spot under the basket and waved his hands. Otto was deep in three-point territory. There were only seven seconds left in the quarter.

Otto quickly put up an off-balance jumper off his left foot that Will knew didn't have a prayer of going in. The ball bounced off the rim with a loud clang and into the hands of one of the Hornets' guards. He ran it down the court for a layup just as the buzzer sounded.

"Sampton ten, Harrison six," the loud-speaker announced.

Will glared at Otto. "I was wide open, Otto," he said. "I was right under the basket."

"Shut up, moron," Otto spat back. "The clock was running down. I had to do something."

"Yeah, but you could have looked for a pass instead of taking a lame shot, *moron*."

"What, are you the coach now? You're a rookie. And for your information, Hopwood, rookies are supposed to keep their mouths shut and learn from the rest of the team. Got it?"

*Not from this team,* Will thought, but he didn't say anything. Things were never like this on the Bulls. Suddenly a 10–6 lead didn't seem so big.

The Slashers were only able to score two baskets during the second quarter. The Hornets' zone defense ran time off the clock and forced the Slashers to take long outside shots.

The Hornets, on the other hand, gained some offensive momentum. When the halftime buzzer sounded, the score was tied at 14.

"What the heck is going on out there?"
Coach White barked at them in the locker
room. "Haven't you heard a thing I've said
to you all week? That's some of the sloppi-
est basketball I've ever seen. Don't take
any more stupid outside shots, understand? Get the ball inside. Pass it! And
crash the boards. You're playing defense
like a bunch of five-year-olds."

Will stared at the locker-room floor while
Coach White shouted at them. No matter
how badly the Bulls had played—and there
were some *bad* games—Coach McBane had
never yelled as Coach White was yelling
now. But then again, Coach McBane hadn't
had to deal with people like Otto Meyerson.
Maybe yelling was the only way to get
through to the Slashers.

"I know we can beat these losers, but we
have to make our own breaks today. We're
playing at home, but no one is going to

38

help you out there." Coach White pointed his scrawny, pale finger toward the court. "So let's stop messing around. Let's do it!"

The Slashers filed silently back into the gym.

"Yo, show 'em what's up, Hopwood!" shouted Brian when Will walked onto the court. "Take 'em to town."

"Show time!" Dave yelled.

Will looked up and forced a weak smile. Dave and Brian looked as if they were itching to play. He knew he couldn't let Coach White and the Slashers get him down. After all, he *was* on a team with some really good players, even if they were jerks.

Suddenly Will was determined to have a great second half. He would prove to the Slashers and to everyone else in that gym how good he was. Not just any old good. Slammin', jammin', in-your-face good. The best center in the league.

"Let's go, Slashers!" he yelled before the buzzer sounded.

Otto dribbled the ball quickly, faked a pass, then sunk a jump shot from the left side of the baseline. "Time out!" he yelled.

Will put his hands on his knees and breathed deeply. A few drops of sweat fell from his face onto the court. The Slashers were down 34–32, and there was less than a minute left in the game.

He walked over to the rest of the Slashers, who were crowding around the bench. Coach White was holding a small chalkboard with a picture of a basketball court on it.

"All right, I know we've been playing man-to-man all game, but now I want to switch to the zone." He drew five X's on the chalk-board in a two–one–two zone formation.

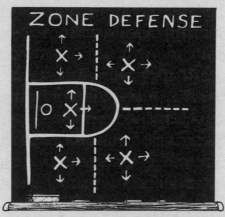

"The zone has worked for the Hornets—so it's gonna work for us. Just don't let them get the ball inside. Force them to shoot from the outside. Spider, the second you see them take a shot, head down-court." He drew an arrow from one of the X's to the opposite basket.

"So far, the Hornets have made most of their baskets from inside the lane," he went on. "We know their outside shooting stinks. So, Will, you get the rebound and feed Spider the long pass. Then go into a full-court press on defense and make sure you hold them in the backcourt until the clock runs out. Then we'll worry about overtime. Got it?"

Will nodded. He just hoped he could get the rebound—if the Hornets took an outside shot. With so little time left in the game, there was no telling what the Hornets would do. The whole plan seemed pretty risky to him.

But when the Hornets inbounded the ball, Will could tell they were confused. The sudden switch to a zone threw them off. They kept looking to penetrate inside, but every time they tried, the Slashers closed the gap.

*"De-fense, de-fense, de-fense . . ."*

Finally one of the Hornets' guards put up an outside shot. It was an air ball that landed right in Will's hands.

By the time Will looked downcourt, Spider was already halfway to the basket. Will hurled the ball to him. Spider dribbled behind his back and sunk a reverse layup.

The crowd exploded. Will couldn't believe it! It was just like the shot Dave had taken during the rematch of the championship—only Spider had made it!

Suddenly Will heard Dave's angry voice booming out of the stands. "Yo, Spider, you copycat! Too stupid to come up with your own moves?"

Spider turned to look at Dave as the rest of the Slashers went into a full-court press.

"Spider!" Will called. "Watch out!"

The Hornets inbounded the ball right past Spider. Before Will knew what was happening, the Hornets had beaten the Slashers on a three-on-one fast break.

"Sampton thirty-four, Harrison thirty-six," announced the loudspeaker.

Will looked at the clock. There were

only fifteen seconds left in the game. He tried to wave the Slashers into a huddle.

"What are you doing, Hopwood?" Otto asked as he dribbled the ball downcourt. "What did I tell you? Rookies are supposed to keep their mouths shut. We don't have time for this."

Will knew he couldn't let Otto bring him down.

"Otto, I'm going to stay to your right. When we hit the top of the key, I'll stand next to the Hornets' guard and set a pick. Fake to your left—then come around me to the right. You'll have a path down the lane."

Otto didn't say anything. He just shot Will a dirty look.

When they reached the top of the key, Will tried to set the pick. But instead of coming around Will to the right, Otto tried to go left. He ran straight into the Hornets' guard and center. They double-teamed him, trapping him far from the basket.

Otto put up an air ball as the sound of the buzzer filled the gym.

"Final score: Sampton thirty-four, Harrison thirty-six."

Will quickly headed toward the locker room. He wanted to avoid seeing Brian and Dave. He was too mad and embarrassed.

He heard the spectators groan as they filed out of the gym. Will gritted his teeth. He could tell that the fans were just as angry and disappointed as he was. The Slashers should have won the game. They *would* have won the game, if Spider hadn't been distracted by Dave's comment. But Will couldn't be angry with Dave. The Slashers would have won if they had played like a team.

But the Slashers weren't a real team. They were just a bunch of jerks who all wore the same uniforms.

*And I'm one of them,* Will thought.

# CHAPTER 6

Dave dribbled the ball a couple of times and squinted in the late-afternoon sun at the basket.

"It's the final seconds of the NBA championship," he said in a loud, deep voice. "Five-time MVP and all-time leading scorer David Danzig has the ball near the top of the key. *Three, two, one* . . ." He put up a jump shot. It bounced off the backboard with a loud bang.

"And Danzig throws a brick," Brian continued. "The angry crowd of twenty thousand pegs him with rotten eggs."

Dave frowned as Brian chased down the ball and thundered back toward the basket, sinking a left-handed layup. "Simmons makes the clutch shot," Brian shouted. He threw both hands into the air. "The crowd goes wild!"

Brian's words echoed over the empty playground.

"Hey—it's getting kinda late," Dave finally said in his normal voice. "Feel like going to Bowman's?"

"Sure." Brian grabbed the ball. "I wonder if Will is out from practice yet."

"I doubt it," said Dave, thinking about how Will had stormed off the court after the Slashers had played the Hornets. He and Brian hadn't seen Will since then—and that was five days ago. "He's had to stay late every day this week," Dave went on. "I guess Coach White is really mad about blowing that first game against Harrison."

"Who wouldn't be? Harrison stinks. The Slashers should have walked all over them."

Dave grinned. "Well, what do you expect? Except for Will, the average Slasher's IQ is about the same as his shoe size." He grabbed the ball from Brian and dribbled through his legs as they crossed the street. "But as Otto said, you have to deal with it."

"Droopy and Fadeaway," Mr. Bowman announced when Dave and Brian opened the front door of Bowman's. "The future of the NBA."

"That's right," put in Nate, who was stocking shelves in the back. "The future of NBA sideline service. When I'm a big star, these boys will be right there with me, making sure all my towels are clean and fresh."

"Gee, you're funny, Nate," Brian said.

"Ever thought about being a comedian?"

"Yeah, but I can't." Nate flashed them a smile. "The NBA would never forgive me."

Mr. Bowman rolled his eyes. "Wise guy," he muttered. Brian and Dave set a couple of Cokes on the counter in front of him. "Tough day on the courts, fellas?" he asked.

Brian shrugged. "Sure—if you think a couple of hours of shooting around alone on an empty playground is tough."

"Hmmm." Mr. Bowman rubbed his chin. "You guys aren't still sore about the Bulls, are you?"

"A little," Brian admitted.

Dave looked out the front window at the playground. "It was bad enough saying good-bye to the twins and Coach McBane. Now Will's not around either. It just stinks not being able to play on a team."

"Hey, from what I hear about Too Tall, playing on a team doesn't sound so hot," Nate said. "Jim told me he doesn't get home from practice until seven—and when he does, he's too tired to do anything except eat and go to bed."

"Sounds to me like that could be bad news," Mr. Bowman added, shaking his head.

Dave knew that Mr. Bowman and Nate were trying to cheer him up. But nothing they could say would bring the Bulls back.

"We've hardly seen Will at all since he joined the Slashers," Dave grumbled, taking a sip of his Coke. "Jim took us to the first game, but Will didn't even want to talk to us when it was over."

"Sounds pretty bad," Mr. Bowman said. "You gotta hand it to him, though—he's sticking with it."

Dave shrugged. "He wants to play team ball."

"And you guys do, too, right?"

Dave nodded.

"You know, when I was your age," Mr. Bowman said, "we didn't have a league around here like you guys do now."

"Uh-oh." Nate's voice came from the back of the store. "Sounds like the beginning of another one of those boring 'When I was your age' stories."

"As I was saying," Mr. Bowman continued,

lowering his eyebrows, "my buddies and I decided to start our own summer league— just for kids our age."

"What did you do?" Dave asked.

"Well, the first thing we did was gather up all the kids we knew in our neighborhood who played basketball. We had about three teams right there. Then we all walked around to different schools and put up signs that said: *'Summer Basketball League forming. Need Players.'*"

Mr. Bowman sighed and looked out the window. "As a matter of fact, we held the tryouts right here at Jefferson. It was a long, long time ago. Seems like yesterday, though."

"Did a lot of kids show up?" Dave was suddenly interested.

"Yeah." Mr. Bowman chuckled. "The place was packed. Most of them didn't know a thing about hoops, though."

"Sounds like the Sampton tryouts," Brian mumbled.

"Anyway, we were able to form a league with six teams," Mr. Bowman continued. "We played every weekend. It was a lot of fun. We even got my dad to ref the games."

"That *really* sounds like Sampton," Brian said, nudging Dave.

But Dave wasn't listening. He suddenly had an idea. "I wonder how many kids would show if *we* put up signs," he said.

"What do you mean?" Brian asked.

"I mean, what do you think would happen if we put up signs all over Branford that said: *Branford Bulls basketball team re-forming. Tryouts at Jefferson Park this Saturday at 1 P.M.?*"

"Are you serious?"

"Why not?" Dave said. "I bet if we did all the work and got a whole team together, the league would let us back in. I bet we could even convince the league to find a coach for us."

"I don't know . . ." Brian sounded doubtful.

Dave grinned. "C'mon, it's worth a shot. I mean, it's not like we have anything to lose. What's the worst that can happen? We find a bunch of kids we can play hoops with."

"Tell you what, fellas." Mr. Bowman leaned across the counter. "If you guys make that sign, I'll make a bunch of copies for you—enough to put one up on every street corner in Branford."

"Now we're talking!" Dave felt excited—like the way he felt right before a big game. "It's Wednesday. If we make the sign tonight and get it copied tomorrow morning, we'll have it all over Branford by Thursday afternoon. That's plenty of time for a Saturday tryout!"

"Well, what are you waiting for?" Mr. Bowman asked with a smile. "Hop to it!"

"I think we should start by putting signs up around Jefferson," Dave said as he and Brian left Bowman's. "A lot of kids besides us shoot hoops there."

"Yeah, that's a good idea," Brian agreed. "And we should put some around—"

"Yo, guys, hold up a sec!"

Dave and Brian turned around. Nate was following close behind them.

"What's up?" Dave asked. "Did we forget something?"

Nate chewed on his lower lip. "Well—not exactly."

Dave looked at Brian. "What's going on, Nate?"

"Look, you guys want to start up the Bulls again, right?"

Dave and Brian nodded.

"But you need to have tryouts. Now, tryouts can be a big mess, see. Kids running around, nobody knows what's going on, everybody's yelling and screaming . . . unless, of course, you have organization. And to have organization, you need an organizer. Somebody with experience. Somebody who can dunk the ball." He grinned. "See what I'm getting at?"

"Are you offering to help us with the tryouts?" Brian asked.

"I'm offering to do more than that, Fadeaway," Nate said. "I'll run the tryouts—and if you guys get a team together, I'll coach the new Branford Bulls."

Wow! Dave couldn't believe it. Nate Bowman wanted to coach the Branford Bulls? It seemed too good to be true.

"What's in it for you?" Brian asked, suspicious.

"Yeah, I thought you had to work with your father all summer," Dave said.

Nate glanced back at his father's store. "Well, I bet if he knew I was keeping you scrubs out of trouble, he'd give me some time off. Anyway, I'd go crazy being cooped up all summer long." He smiled. "Plus, it'll give me a chance to work on my game, too."

"That makes sense," Dave said. He shook Nate's hand. "You're hired."

"Only thing is, though, I know I *have* to help my dad in the store on some days. I wouldn't be able to make it to every single practice."

"Maybe the league can get somebody else to help out when you aren't there," Dave suggested.

Nate nodded. "Or you guys could practice on your own. On second thought, that might not be such a great idea. . . ."

"What about Jim Hopwood?" Brian said. "He could probably help us out."

"Fadeaway, my man—you're brilliant!" Nate rapped on his head with his fist. "Why didn't I think of that? It's perfect! I know Jim is looking for something to do—and this is right down his alley."

"You really think the league will go for it?" Dave said excitedly.

"Dave, don't you worry about a thing." Nate looked over at the playground and rubbed his hands together. "Just get those signs up. Jim and I will take it from there."

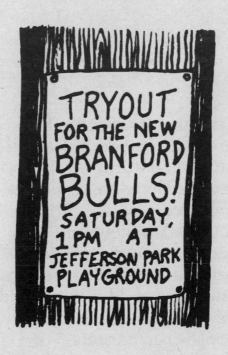

## CHAPTER 7

Dave's mom dropped him off at Jefferson Park playground a little before 1:00 P.M. on Saturday afternoon. He wanted to get there early, before the try-outs got started.

Dave couldn't believe his eyes. He had never seen so many people packed onto a basketball court at the same time. There were boys, girls, toddlers, tall kids, short kids, kids who looked old enough to be in high school—even parents.

And all of them were running, shooting, laughing, and shouting at the top of their lungs. It was a mess.

Then he spotted Brian, who was standing in the middle of the court, looking lost and confused.

"Brian!" Dave shouted. "Over here!"

Brian turned in Dave's direction and came running over with a relieved look on his face. "Can you believe it?" he asked, shaking his head. "This is nuts!"

Dave started laughing. "I guess we put up those signs in all the right places."

"I guess," Brian said. "But what are we going to do? I mean how are we going to have tryouts? Most of these people can't play on our team."

Just then Todd and Allie, Brian's seven-year-old twin brother and sister, came running over. "Let's go, Brian!" Todd shouted. "Let's play!"

Brian looked at Dave. "See what I mean?"

"What's up, guys?" Dave asked, slapping their hands. "You aren't here for the tryouts, are you?"

"We sure are," Todd said. "Hoops runs in the family."

Allie started giggling.

"Uh-oh," Dave said. "I think we're in big trouble."

"You got that right," said a familiar voice behind them.

Dave turned around. Will was standing behind him in his Slashers uniform. He had a big grin on his face.

"Will! What's up, man?" Dave hadn't expected Will to show up. "Long time no see!"

"Yeah, I know," Will said, suddenly avoiding Dave's eyes. "I haven't been around much. I've been pretty busy over in Sampton."

"Yeah, we heard," Brian said. "How's it going over there?"

"Oh, it's okay." Will shrugged. He looked around the playground. "Jim told me you guys were having tryouts today—I never thought this many people would show up. I thought I'd come check it out before I went to practice."

"Yeah, I guess we should try to get things organized a little bit before Nate gets here," Dave said.

Suddenly a basketball came whizzing past Dave's head. The twins tried running after it and crashed into him.

"Looks like you're going to have your

hands full," Will said in a gloomy voice. "I guess I'll get going. Coach White hates it when anybody's late." He turned and bolted out of the front gate.

Dave looked at Brian.

"You thinking what I'm thinking?" Brian asked.

"If you're thinking that Will is more bummed than ever that he's playing with Otto instead of us—then yes."

"I guess it doesn't help that we're trying to put the Bulls back together, either. Or that Will's brother is gonna be coaching us."

Dave shook his head. He hadn't really thought about it like that before. "That *is* kinda harsh."

Dave and Brian made their way to the half-court line, stepping around people and ducking flying balls.

"All right, people!" Brian shouted. "Let's stop shooting around."

Nobody responded. Balls kept flying at the hoop, and everyone kept screaming.

"*People!*" Brian shouted again.

Dave laughed. "I don't think anybody can hear you, man."

But then, out of the corner of his eye, Dave noticed Nate and Jim walking through the front gate of the playground. They were both wearing their high school team uniforms. Jim was holding a ball. Even from far away, Nate's black high-top Nikes looked incredibly huge.

Dave saw Jim nodding in the direction of the basket. Then Nate smiled. He began sprinting toward it, snaking his way through the mob of people.

When Nate reached the lane, Jim threw the ball up. Nate leaped high into the air, caught the ball, and slammed it through the hoop.

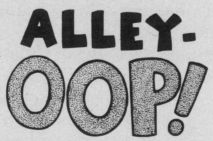

The crowd went absolutely silent.

Nate held on to the rim for a few seconds, swinging in the air. Then he

60

dropped lightly to the ground. "All right, everybody, let's get started," he said calmly, clapping his hands. Jim came and stood next to him.

Everyone quickly formed a circle around the two coaches.

Dave and Brian were still standing at mid-court. They glanced at each other. "Somehow I don't think we could have gotten everybody organized as quickly as Nate did," Brian whispered.

"Nope," said Dave. He grinned. "I think these coaches are gonna work out real nice."

CHAPTER 8

"All right, first things first," Nate said. "This team is for ten- and eleven-year-olds. I'm sorry to say that anybody who isn't ten or eleven won't be able to try out."

A groan went up from a group of young kids standing around Todd and Allie.

"Can we stay and watch?" Todd asked.

Nate grinned. "Of course you can, little man. But I'm gonna have to ask you all to stay on the sidelines."

Slowly people started clearing the court. About ten kids were left standing around Nate and Jim underneath the basket.

"All right, then," Nate went on. "Behind

you all are the two starters we have so far on the Branford Bulls—Brian Simmons and David Danzig."

Dave and Brian nodded to the rest of the kids.

"We're going to have a little game just to get things started," Jim said. He quickly counted the kids on the court. "Six-on-six. You five play with Dave." He stuck his arm out, dividing the group in half. "The rest of you play with Brian. We'll play to ten."

As Dave ran to the opposite end of the court, he glanced at his teammates. He could tell right away by the confused looks on their faces that some of the kids had hardly ever played basketball.

One kid with a bright mop of red hair kept trying to dribble with both hands. Dave frowned. "You can't do that."

"You can't?"

"No. It's called double dribbling."

The kid shrugged.

But there was one guy who seemed different. He was a tall, skinny African American kid with red, white, and blue wristbands. Dave saw by the way the kid moved that he was obviously at home on the basketball court.

"Everybody pick a man to guard," Nate yelled from the sidelines.

Brian fired a bounce pass at a big chubby kid on his team. But just as the chubby kid was about to catch the ball, the kid with the red, white, and blue wristbands sprinted forward and picked off the pass.

Before anybody knew what was happening, he had thundered down the court and put in a flawless layup off the backboard.

"Nice work!" Jim yelled. "Way to hustle!"

"Great play," Dave said to the kid as they hopped back on defense.

"Thanks a lot." The kid smiled.

"What's your name?"

"Derek Roberts," he said quietly.

"Nice to meet you, Derek."

Brian's team took the ball back downcourt. The chubby kid lumbered into the lane and posted up on Dave. As Dave tried to keep the kid from getting close to the basket, Brian fired the ball. The kid

64

caught the ball, spun, and put up a quick shot over Dave's head.

"Good shot, man," Brian called.

"Thanks. The name's Chunky," said the chubby kid as he loped back on defense. Then he grinned. "But I also answer to 'man.'"

"Give-and-go," Dave whispered to Derek as Derek brought the ball downcourt.

When Derek reached the foul line, he dished the ball off to Dave and headed right down the middle of the lane toward the basket. Dave lobbed the ball in his direction. Derek easily outjumped the two defenders next to him. When he landed, he spun on one foot, pump-faked twice, and swished it.

Brian ran up to Dave as his team

inbounded the ball. "I think we've found our new starting forward," he said, giving Dave a quick low five. "He's the next Michael Jordan!"

Just then a short blond kid with wrap-around glasses put up what looked like a wild shot from three-point territory. It hit the backboard, spun around the rim several times, and finally fell through the net.

"Mark is my name, and hoops is my game," he shouted, winking at the people watching on the sidelines. Everyone started cheering.

"Nice shot, Mark," Brian said.

"Thanks. Nothin' to it."

Dave looked over at the sideline and saw Nate and Jim talking and nodding their heads. Suddenly Jim raised his hands.

"All right, y'all, that's enough."

"Good game, guys, good game," Nate

said, grabbing the ball and stepping into the middle of the court. "Jim and I want to thank everyone for coming down here. You three—Chunky, Mark, and Derek— can you guys stick around for a sec?"

While Jim was rounding up the three of them, Dave and Brian took a seat on the bench. "Things are looking up," Dave said.

"Those guys are pretty good."

"Yo, Droopy, Fadeaway—come over here," Nate called. Brian and Dave walked back onto the court.

"I'd like to formally introduce you to your new teammates," Nate said, smiling.

The two of them shook hands with Chunky, Derek, and Mark.

Nate flashed his wide smile. "I think we have ourselves a starting lineup. I know we don't have any substitutes, but the other kids just weren't ready for organized ball yet. Don't worry, we'll pick up some other players throughout the season. Let's go across the street to my dad's store. Drinks are on me."

The kids slumped on the bench outside the store while Nate and Jim went inside to get sodas. When they came back out, Mr. Bowman was with them.

He was holding a large cardboard box.

"So these are the new Branford Bulls, huh?" he asked. "Well, I guess it's a good thing that I have these, then."

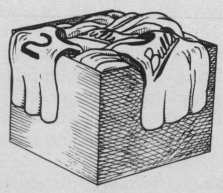

He put the box down in front of the bench. Dave's mouth fell open in shock when he saw what was inside. It was the Bulls' old uniforms!

"Oh, yeah, I guess I forgot to mention to you guys that I talked to the league yesterday," Nate said, grinning. "They let the Bulls back in. We have our first game against Harrison in one week."

Dave and Brian stared at each other as Jim passed sodas out. They were speechless. It was too good to be true.

Jim raised his can. "To the new Branford Bulls!"

# CHAPTER 9

"Listen up, guys," Nate said. "Remember what we worked on this week—working the ball around on the outside with an eye for the man inside. Crisp passes until a hole in the D opens up."

The Bulls were standing in a huddle on the sidelines at the Harrison community center. Dave looked around at the crowd in the bleachers. The big moment had finally arrived. They were just two minutes away from the first game of the season!

"And remember what we talked about when it comes to our own D," Jim added. "Keep them to the outside and—"

*"Crash the boards,"* all five Bulls finished for him.

Nate and Jim glanced at each other and started laughing. "We haven't been repeating ourselves too much, have we, boys?" Nate said, looking around the huddle. "Good. I didn't think so."

They *had* repeated themselves a lot—but Dave didn't mind. Over the past week, the two coaches had been tough in working the new Bulls into shape for the game. But Dave felt that the long practices had been worth it. By the end of the week, the new Bulls were finally starting to play as a team. They were ready.

Just then the buzzer sounded.

"All right, now, boys, put your hands in!" Jim shouted. He stuck his hand in the middle of the huddle.

Dave threw his on top—followed by Brian, then Chunky, then Mark, then Derek, and finally Nate.

*"Show time!"* they all yelled together.

The crowd quieted as Derek faced off

against the Hornets' center for the jump ball. Chunky was going to play center, but he wasn't very good at jump balls.

The ref blew the whistle and tossed the ball up in the air. Derek leaped up and batted it to Mark, who took the ball downcourt.

Dave could tell right away that Mark was nervous. Mark had clowned around a lot during practice. But now that he was on the court, starting as a guard in his first game, he didn't seem so sure of himself. He dribbled carefully, and his eyes, behind his wraparound glasses, were glued to the Hornet who was guarding him.

Mark quickly passed the ball off to Dave, who positioned himself at the top of the key. After looking around, he worked the ball to Derek, who was at his left. Derek immediately passed the ball off to Brian, who was standing below him on the left side of the baseline.

Dave grinned as Brian put up a fadeaway jumper. Brian was shooting from his sweet spot—and it was nothin' but net. Just like the old days.

But the Hornets moved fast on offense.

Their center was a tall, meaty kid with braces. He was at least three inches taller than Chunky, and probably ten pounds lighter. He got the ball inside, faked a pass, and easily drove past Chunky for a quick layup.

"Let's see some tough D, guys!" Jim hollered from the bench.

The next time the Bulls had the ball, Dave launched a lightning-fast bounce pass to Mark, who was standing near the sideline on the right side of the court. Mark fumbled the ball for a second. When he gained control, two Hornets were rushing at him. He threw up a wild shot that went over the top of the backboard.

"Be patient out there, Mark," Nate called to him. "Work the ball around."

"At least work it within three miles of the net," Dave muttered under his breath. He was going to say something out loud, but he stopped himself. Mark was probably having a hard enough time as it was.

The first quarter ended with Harrison leading the Bulls 14–12.

"Look, guys, we know that the Hornets are double-teaming Mark and forcing a lot

of turnovers," Jim said before the second quarter started. "Mark, remember that when they're double-teaming you, it means that Dave is probably open. So be alert. Try to make a pass instead of going for the shot."

At the start of the second quarter, Dave took the ball downcourt. He saw Derek cutting under the basket to the right side of the lane. Derek had his back to the Hornets' center and was open for a pass.

Dave fired the ball at him. Derek caught it and pivoted quickly on his left foot, as if he were turning toward the inside. But just as the Hornets' center jumped up to block him, Derek quickly spun around in the opposite direction and rolled the ball off his fingertips for an underhanded shot—from his *left* hand. It sailed through the net.

"Wow!" Dave said, slapping Derek's

hand as they ran back on defense. "Alonzo Mourning teach you that one?"

Derek just shrugged.

Most of the guys that Dave knew who were as good as Derek were constantly running their mouths—usually about how great they were. But it seemed as if Derek never said a word. Dave didn't mind. Derek really delivered the goods on the court.

Chunky and Mark, on the other hand, were a different story. Chunky proved no match for the tall kid with braces. Not only could the kid outjump Chunky, but if he missed a shot, he usually beat Chunky to the rebound for an easy layup. Derek kept having to leave his own man unguarded to help Chunky on D.

And Mark kept freaking out whenever the Hornets double-teamed him. A few times he was able to pass the ball out to Dave. Twice he was lucky enough to sink jumpers from deep outside.

Most of the time, though, he caused turnovers.

With four minutes left in the second quarter, the Hornets had jumped ahead 24–18.

And the closer the game got to halftime, the more angry and frustrated Dave became. The old Bulls had usually creamed Harrison. Chunky and Mark were not exactly David Robinson and Reggie Miller. *If Will and the twins were playing, things would be different.*

Finally Dave snapped. Mark had the ball on the left side of the court. Instead of looking for an open man inside, he tried throwing the ball back to Dave at the top of the key. The pass was picked off, and suddenly the Hornets were taking the ball downtown on an undefended three-man fast break. Before the Bulls could do anything about it, the score was 26–18.

"Yo, Mark!" Dave shouted, his eyebrows twisting. "What's your problem, man? Are you wearing the wrong goggles or something?"

"Time out!" Nate called from the bench. The Bulls gathered for a huddle.

"Dave—do us all a favor and leave your attitude at Jefferson, okay?" Nate said sternly.

"Sorry," Dave mumbled. He felt bad now. He hadn't really meant to be mean to Mark. He was just mad that the new Bulls weren't playing like the old Bulls.

"Look, guys, I know it's tough out there." Nate's voice softened a little bit. "We've just got to watch for careless mistakes."

"Harrison's a good team," Jim added. "Remember, they beat the Slashers two weeks ago—and the Slashers are the defending champs. Just keep your heads up. Try getting the ball to Brian more. Derek, set picks for Brian to come inside."

Derek and Brian nodded.

"All right, guys, let's show 'em what's up. There's plenty of time left in the half to put some points on the board."

*Let's show 'em what's up.* Will had always said that when the old Bulls were losing. But Will had always played best under pressure.

*He's probably scoring the winning basket for the Slashers right now,* Dave thought glumly, dribbling the ball downcourt.

Dave quickly fed the ball to Chunky,

who faked to Derek, then dished it off to Brian. Derek, who was standing between Brian and the kid with braces, froze in place—preventing the kid from getting to the ball. Brian dashed around the two of them on the inside, banking in a shot off the backboard.

"Nice pick! Now we're talking!" Jim yelled. "Way to go, Bulls!"

Once again, the Hornets quickly brought the ball back before the Bulls had a chance to get their defense set. The kid with braces put up an unguarded shot from the right side of the foul line.

The shot was off—only there weren't any Bulls under the basket to get the rebound. But as the ball hit the rim and bounced up into the air, Dave saw Derek come streaking across the court. His red,  white, and blue wristbands were a blur as he leaped for the ball and snagged it over the heads of two Hornets.

Dave couldn't believe it. The kid was amazing! The gym burst into applause. Derek was so good that even the Hornets' fans were cheering for him.

Derek whipped the ball out to Dave. Suddenly Dave found himself in a three-on-one fast break with Mark and Brian.

Dave passed the ball off to Mark, who threw it ahead to Brian, beating the lone defender. Brian had a clear path to the hoop.

Then Dave saw something that he almost never saw.

Brian missed an unguarded layup.

The ball slammed off the backboard and back toward the middle of the court—right into the hands of the lone Hornet. The halftime buzzer sounded.

"Harrison twenty-six, Branford twenty," the scorekeeper announced.

Things didn't look good for the Bulls. They didn't look good at all.

# CHAPTER 10

Nate and Jim paced silently across the locker-room floor. The five Bulls were slumped in their seats, staring at their feet.

Nate finally stood still. "All right, guys," he said, rubbing his hands together. "We've got our work cut out for us. We've got to come together out there like we did in practice. We've got to prove that we're a team—a good team."

"A *great* team," Jim went on. "The league did us a huge favor by letting us put the Branford Bulls back together after the season already started. We can't let them down."

Dave tried to get himself psyched for

the second half, but he could hardly even catch his breath. Drops of sweat dripped from his forehead onto the floor.

He glanced around the locker room. A great team? Chunky and Mark looked like they were about to pass out. Brian's eyes were closed. Derek was wiping his face with his wristbands.

Dave winced. Having a five-man squad with no subs was taking its toll.

"We're doing our best," Brian finally said, letting out a big sigh. "It's just not the same without Will and the twins and the other guys."

"No, it's not the same, Fadeaway," Nate said with a stern look on his face. "It's not the same at all. That's why it's up to us to forget about the past and concentrate on *right now*. Understand?"

"Nate's right," Jim said. "Thinking about the old Bulls is going to get us nowhere fast. So let's drop it and focus on what we have to get done out there in the second half."

"Okay, then," Nate continued. "The key is defense. You gotta stick to your man like glue. We have to keep them from getting the ball inside, so—"

Nate's speech was suddenly interrupted by a loud knock on the locker-room door. He frowned.

"Come in."

The door swung open.

Dave's eyes nearly popped out of his head.

Will was standing in the doorway, wearing his black Slashers uniform, dripping with sweat, and completely out of breath.

"Will!" Jim cried. "What the heck are you doing here? I thought you guys were playing Essex today!"

"Canceled my contract," Will gasped between breaths.

"What?"

"I'm not on the Slashers anymore," he finally managed.

"Will, what are you talking about?"

Will stumbled into the locker room and fell into an empty seat next to Dave. "Well, even after beating Essex today, I realized that I'd rather give up basketball for good than have to spend another second with Otto." He grinned. "And giving up hoops isn't an option."

Dave laughed. "I bet Otto could make Hakeem Olajuwon want to give up hoops."

"So when the game was over, I told them I was quitting," Will went on. "Only Coach White seemed surprised and a little disappointed. The rest of the team actually seemed kinda psyched." He cocked his eyebrow. "Anyway, I got outta there, hopped on a bus, and got myself down here as fast as I could."

Jim's lips slowly began curling up in a smile. "Oh, yeah? Now, why did you do that?"

Will looked around the room. "Look, guys, I know I missed tryouts and everything. But now I'm a free agent. And if you guys will have me, I'd like to join the Branford Bulls. Uh, right this second—if that's okay with you."

Nate started laughing. "Right this second, Too Tall? Man, you free agents drive a hard bargain. But I'll tell you what, you're hired. Welcome to the Branford Bulls."

Together Dave and Brian exploded with a huge *"Yesss!"* They jumped up to run toward Will.

"Whoa, hold on a sec, boys," Nate said. "First things first. We gotta get Will out of that ugly uniform. And I have just the thing. Be right back."

Nate bolted from the locker room. Dave introduced Will to Mark, Derek, and Chunky.

"Man, am I glad you showed up," Chunky said. "If I had to play another second, I'd probably die."

Nate burst back through the door, holding Will's old uniform. "My dad tossed this in my trunk," he said, flashing his smile. "Hope it still fits, Too Tall."

Just then the buzzer sounded on the court. The second half was starting in two minutes. They filed out of the locker room.

"The Branford Bulls have a late arrival," the scorekeeper announced. "Coming in at center, number fourteen, Will Hopwood!"

Will was pumped. The crowd in Harrison slowly quieted as Will faced off against the tall kid with braces for the jump ball. Even though he had already played a full game with the Slashers that day, he didn't feel tired at all.

*Time to crush the Hornets,* Will said to himself as he tensed for the jump. *This time it's gonna be a piece of cake.*

He sprang straight up and smacked the ball to Dave.

As Dave took the ball downcourt, Will headed toward the left side of the lane, trying to shake the kid with braces. Dave and Mark worked the ball around the perimeter.

Will could see that they wanted to pass inside, so he positioned himself closer to the basket. The kid with braces had his eye on the ball, too.

After a few seconds, Will bolted across the lane to the right side of the hoop. Dave launched the ball at him. But the kid with braces saw the pass coming. Will suddenly found himself trapped by the kid under the basket, unable to make a shot.

Out of the corner of his eye, he saw Derek fake to the outside. It was just enough to gain a few steps on the Hornet who was covering him.

The timing was perfect. Just as the kid with braces tried to swat the ball away from him, Will threw a low bounce pass under the kid's hands.

Derek swept it up and laid it into the basket.

# TWO POINTS!

"Yo, that was *pretty*!" Chunky shouted from the sideline.

The Bulls were now only two baskets away from a tie game. If they could keep the Hornets from getting the ball inside, Will was pretty sure the Bulls could prevent them from scoring. Will knew from the Slashers' game against the Hornets that their outside shooting was weak.

Unfortunately, though, the Hornets' biggest strength was their passing.

The next time the Hornets got the ball, one of their guards dribbled around the top of the key and went up for what looked like a jump shot. But instead of shooting, he passed the ball over Mark's head to the kid with braces.

Luckily, Will was standing in the middle of the lane between the kid and the basket. As the kid put up a shot, Will tried to stuff him—and accidentally swatted the kid's arm.

85

# SCREECH!

The harsh sound of the ref's whistle filled the gym. Will turned around just in time to see the ball wobble around the rim and fall into the net.

"Basket counts!" shouted the ref.

Will's head dropped to his chest and he stomped his foot on the ground. What a stupid mistake!

"Don't sweat it, Will," Brian said as they lined up on opposite sides of the lane for the free throw. "We've got plenty of time."

The kid with braces dribbled the ball a couple of times at the free-throw line and stared at the basket.

The gym was perfectly still.

Finally he spun the ball in his hands, lifted it, and let it fly off his fingertips.

The crowd exploded. *"Hor-nets, Hor-nets, Hor-nets . . ."*

86

Will grabbed the ball and inbounded it to Mark. The score was now 29–22. Will put the three-point play behind him.

He knew he couldn't let the Bulls down. It was time to play team ball and get the job done in the clutch—as he always had.

Mark took the ball down the court and passed it off to Dave. Will moved into the center of the lane, then quickly back out again, managing to get open on the right side of the court.

Dave dished the ball to him. Will turned and faced the basket. He hesitated for a second. Before he knew it, two Hornets were double-teaming him.

Out of the corner of his eye, he saw Derek shake his man. Will managed to get off a bounce pass. Derek instantly fired up a lucky hook shot that banked in off the backboard.

"Unbelievable!" Jim shouted from the bench.

Will knew he wouldn't be able to count on Derek to bail him out of every shaky situation—and the Bulls were still behind by five.

Over the next two quarters, he made three baskets, had two assists, and pulled down an amazing seven rebounds. But it still wasn't enough to give the Bulls the lead.

The score was 45–44, Harrison. The Hornets had the ball and were trying to run out the clock.

Somehow, Will knew, he had to force a turnover. The seconds were ticking away.

Just when the crowd started counting down the last ten seconds, Will saw his opportunity. He had noticed that one of the Hornets' guards always tossed to his right during a stall. When the kid got the ball, Will anticipated his pass, then lunged forward for the steal.

The crowd gasped as Will ran the ball downcourt. *"Eight, seven, six . . ."*

One of their guards had managed to put himself between Will and the basket.

*"Five, four, three . . ."*

Will heard the footsteps of the rest of the players pounding down the court behind him. His heart galloped. This was it!

*"Two, one . . ."*

Will stopped short, and then leaped into the air, letting the ball roll off his fingers at the height of his jump.

The sound of the buzzer filled the gym

as the ball sailed toward the basket. Will held his breath . . .

*"Yesssss!"*

The next thing he knew, Will was being mauled by his teammates, his brother, and Nate. They lifted him high into the air over the court.

"Too Tall Hopwood!" Nate cried. "Clutch player of the year!"

Hearing those words, Will threw his arms over his head. He had done his job against Harrison. The Bulls had played team ball. They were back on the road to the championship!

*Now it's time to take care of the rest of the league,* he said to himself.

"Show time!"